MINI RABBIT
Come Home

4
ELLIE
X

First published in hardback by HarperCollins *Children's Books* in 2021

1 3 5 7 9 10 8 6 4 2

HB ISBN: 978-0-00-826493-2
PB ISBN: 978-0-00-826494-9

HarperCollins *Children's Books* is a division of HarperCollins*Publishers* Ltd.
1 London Bridge Street, London SE1 9GF
www.harpercollins.co.uk
HarperCollins*Publishers*, 1st Floor, Watermarque Building,
Ringsend Road, Dublin 4, Ireland

Text and illustrations copyright © John Bond 2021

Printed in China

MINI RABBIT
Come Home

JOHN BOND

HarperCollins *Children's Books*

Mother Rabbit and Mini Rabbit
are setting up a camp in the garden.

Mini Rabbit has been looking
forward to this day all week.

This is going to be the BEST day EVER!

Mini Rabbit is very, very excited.

Can I build the DEN?

Can I toast the MARSHMALLOWS?

Can I stay up REALLY late?

Yes, Mini Rabbit,
we just need a
few last things.

Mother Rabbit has made a list of the things they need.

Okay, Mini Rabbit.

But don't take too long –
the weather's not
looking very good.

First stop, the sweet shop.

Hello there, Mini Rabbit,

what can I get for you?
Would you like some ice cream?

No, thank you.

I am CAMPING
and we need some
marshmallows.

We need LOTS OF marshmallows!

Mini Rabbit needs to make sure those marshmallows get back to camp safely.

These
scoff
scoff
are the
BEST
marshmallows
EVER!

Well, I'm sure one or two won't be missed.

Next stop, the farmyard.

Hello.
I am camping and I need
to make a BIG DEN
and I need to borrow
some rope, please?

No problem,
Mini Rabbit.
How much do you need?

Ummm.
A LOT.

Looks like Mini Rabbit will definitely be able
to make a very good den with that!

This will be the
BIGGEST,
BEST
DEN
EVER!

Now Mini Rabbit just needs to collect some wood for the campfire.

Hello, Mini Rabbit.

Do you need a hand with anything?

Yes, please. I need some WOOD for our campfire.

This one is GOOD.

Well. That's everything on the list.
Mini Rabbit should probably head back
to camp quickly, before it gets too late.

This . . .   is going to be . .

LOOK.
I got everything!

We just need to tie that down.
Now, where was the rope,
Mini Rabbit?

Ummm . . .

ERRR . . .

I don't need rope.

SEE!

I'm sure that won't
blow away . . .

Time to start
the campfire.

Mini Rabbit –
were there not any
smaller logs?
This one might take
a while to light.

Errr.
I'll get the marshmall— OH!

Oh dear. Looks like the marshmallows are all gone . . .

And it's not looking like the best weather for camping any more.

Why don't you come home now, Mini Rabbit?
It's not going to be very much fun out here.

NO, no. I won't come home.
I need to stay up late
and sleep in my den.

This is meant to be the

BEST

day

EVER!

Oh, there you are, Mini Rabbit.
How's the camp?

My den broke.

The campfire went out.

And there were
no marshmallows left.

It was the WORST
camp
EVER . . .

Never mind, Mini Rabbit.

Look what I made.

Hmm.

That is quite a good den,
I suppose . . .